Butterwings

Written and illustrated
by Robin James

A Serendipity™ Book

PSS!
PRICE STERN SLOAN

The Serendipity™ Series was created by Stephen Cosgrove and Robin James.

Published by Price Stern Sloan, Inc.,
a member of Penguin Putnam Books for Young Readers, New York.

Printed in Singapore. Published simultaneously in Canada.

Library of Congress Catalog Card Number: 93-63055
ISBN 0-8431-3920-X

Revised Edition
2000 Printing

Dedicated to Autumn Rowe, whose friendship and love of horses helped this story come to be.

—Robin

Beyond the highest mountains, where the soft, red blush of spring spreads across the sloping hills, there is a beautiful place called Wingsong. It is a magical place, for it is where all the tiny winged horses are born.

One of these magical little horses was a bright, golden palomino called Glitterby. She had a thick, snowy-white mane and tail that snapped in the wind as she frolicked about the meadow. She was a very happy horse because she was with foal and soon to become a mother.

One morning Glitterby awoke with a strange, quivering feeling, and she realized that the day had arrived for her new baby to enter the world. She told the other mares as she headed off to the forest. They smiled with joy and anticipation, knowing that she would be returning soon with a tiny one by her side.

Later that evening, as the moonlight began to glimmer on the swaying grasses of the valley, the grazing mares snapped to attention. There was Glitterby emerging from the forest, with the tall grass mysteriously moving a few feet behind her.

As Glitterby slowly approached, the beautiful evening light unveiled her new baby, a tiny version of herself with golden wings and a velvety pink muzzle.

"What's her name?" one of the mares asked.

Glitterby giggled and said, "You know that clumsy little butterfly everyone calls Butterfingers? Right after my baby was born, he landed on her back. There he sat, resting his chin in his hands, admiring her, until he fell asleep and slid off with a plop on the ground! I thought it was so cute that I named her Butterwings!"

With love in their hearts, all the mares of Wingsong gathered around the new mother and baby as they nestled down for the night.

As morning broke, Glitterby gently woke her tiny baby and helped her to her feet. Delighted with life, Butterwings playfully tossed her head and tried out her wobbly new legs. She hopped up and down with glee and wheeled and reared, playing with Butterfingers and all the other butterflies of the meadow as they danced around her. Her tiny whinny could be heard, talking about such important things as sunshine, buttercups and the colors of the meadow.

Day after day, Butterwings slowly ventured farther and farther away from her mother, just wanting to explore, watch and listen to every new experience of life. One day, as she was playing with the butterflies, one landed gently on her back and began to laugh hysterically. She turned her head around to see what was so funny and noticed he was pointing at her tail.

"What's so funny?" Butterwings asked. But the butterfly couldn't stop laughing long enough to answer.

Well, Butterwings couldn't see anything funny, and was getting a little miffed at this butterfly's rudeness. So she shook him off with a flick of her hind leg. A few moments later, she heard several tiny voices laughing behind her. Hovering over her was a group of butterflies giggling their heads off. She looked again, and this time strained her neck as far as she could. To her shock and dismay, she finally saw what all the fuss was about. There, on her rump, and all around her tail, were at least a dozen big, round and very-hard-to-miss purple spots!

"Oh no!" Butterwings thought to herself. "How could this be?" She stared in amazement. "I must find a way to get rid of these horrible purple spots. How did this happen?" Suddenly her wonderful, carefree joy gave way to a serious determination. She just had to find a way to rid herself of those awful spots.

Butterwings raced to the river and waded in over her back. "This will do it!" she said, letting the water run over her. When she felt she had soaked long enough to wash off the spots, she jumped out of the river onto the bank. With a huge spray of water drops, she shook herself dry.

Slowly, she turned to look. Those silly purple things were still there!

"I know," she thought, "I'll lie in the sun and bleach them out!" Convinced that her new plan would work, Butterwings chose a nice spot in the grass, and with a confident smile, she lay down for a nap. The purple spots were facing right into the afternoon sun.

A few hours later, Butterwings awoke, got to her feet with a yawn and a stretch, and looked behind her. "Oh no!" she said loudly. The spots were still there. "Now what am I going to do? I'm never going to get rid of these terrible things!"

Butterwings walked over to the nearest big tree with scratchy bark and tried rubbing those darn spots off. She would have been there all night if she hadn't been summoned by her mother and the other mares. They gathered around her and all started speaking at once.

"Oh, Butterwings, hurry. There's something you must see!"

The other horses were so insistent that she forgot about her spots, and curiously followed them to the edge of the meadow. Butterwings eagerly hurried to the front of the group.

As Butterwings stepped forward and looked down, she saw the most beautiful sight she had ever seen. It was a tiny, glistening black filly. She had four white socks, a white blaze and wait . . . something else. There, on her rump, and all around her tail, were at least a dozen big, round and very-hard-to-miss purple spots!

Butterwings couldn't believe it! The curious thing was that no one seemed to notice. And no one was laughing. Butterwings was absolutely baffled.

"Don't you see those—" She was accidentally bumped out of the way by everyone trying to see. "You mean, you don't mind those—"

"Those what?" her mother asked as she nuzzled her close.

"You know, those . . . things on her back. They're just like mine. The ones that the butterflies were all laughing at."

Glitterby smiled and said, "Butterwings, you're getting as silly as the butterflies."

Suddenly Butterwings heard the familiar sound of laughter from several tiny voices. She looked down at the new filly. Hovering over her was a group of butterflies giggling their heads off. But from where she was standing, she could see something else, too. The butterflies looked as though they were pointing right at the filly's tail, but on the ground she saw what they were really laughing at. The funny little clumsy butterfly had fallen down again and was laughing at himself the hardest of all!

Butterwings looked up at her mother and realized how silly she was to think that the butterflies had been laughing at her.

From that day forward, Butterwings proudly pranced in the meadows of Wingsong, growing everyday and secretly showing off her beautiful purple spots. She realized that every baby born in the land, with spots or no spots, was loved just as they are.

WHEN IT SEEMS THAT SOMEONE
IS LAUGHING RIGHT AT YOU
IT MIGHT BE A JOKE
THAT YOU COULD LAUGH AT TOO.

Serendipity™ Books

Created by
Stephen Cosgrove and Robin James

Enjoy all the delightful books in the Serendipity™ Series:

BANGALEE
BUTTERMILK
BUTTERMILK-BEAR
BUTTERWINGS
CATUNDRA
CRABBY GABBY
CRICKLE-CRACK
DRAGOLIN
THE DREAM TREE
FANNY
FEATHER FIN
FLUTTERBY
FRAZZLE
GABBY
THE GNOME FROM NOME
GRAMPA-LOP
THE GRUMPLING
HUCKLEBUG
JINGLE BEAR
LADY ROSE
LEO THE LOP
LEO THE LOP (TAIL TWO)
LEO THE LOP (TAIL THREE)
MAUI-MAUI
MAYNARD'S MERMAID
MEMILY
MING LING
MISTY MORGAN
MORGAN AND ME
MORGAN AND YEW
MORGAN MORNING
MUMKIN
NITTER PITTER
PERSNICKITY
POPPYSEED
RAZ-MA-TAZ
RHUBARB
SASSAFRAS
SERENDIPITY
SNIFFLES
SQUEAKERS
TRAPPER

PSS!
PRICE STERN SLOAN